This
Birthday Book
was presented to
St. Joseph
School Library
in honor of
the birthday of
Justin
Mezo
9-23-89

Text and illustrations copyright © 1992 by Jan Bačkovský
First published in Great Britain by ABC, All Books for Children,
a division of The All Children's Company Ltd.
Inquiries should be addressed to Tambourine Books,
a division of William Morrow & Company, Inc.,
1350 Avenue of the Americas, New York, New York 10019.
Printed in Hong Kong

Library of Congress Cataloging in Publication data
was not available in time for publication of this book, but can
be obtained from the Library of Congress
ISBN 0-688-11857-7 (trade)   ISBN 0-688-11858-5 (lib.)
L.C. Number 91-47930
1   3   5   7   9   10   8   6   4   2
First U.S. edition

Jan Bačkovský

TROUBLE IN PARADISE

TAMBOURINE BOOKS · New York

Mr. Smith was a famous big game hunter.

He was getting ready
to go on one of his famous
big game hunting trips.

"I am about to become the first person to set foot on Paradise Island," he boasted. "I'll catch lots of animals there."
Mr. Smith was very happy.

He spent his
journey relaxing.

The animals on Paradise Island saw Mr. Smith on TV so they knew he was on his way. They spent their time thinking of ways to welcome him.

So when Mr. Smith's ship was near the island
the whale lashed the water with her tail.

Mr. Smith slid this way...

and that way...

and landed with a BUMP!

Mr. Smith stepped ashore.
He wasn't very happy. In fact,
he was very unhappy. His head hurt.
But Mr. Smith set out to hunt.

The parrot saw him and flew off to tell the
lion. "He's here! He's here!" she squawked.

"Oh! What a beautiful butterfly!
I must have it!" Mr. Smith cried.
He started to feel happier.

"Grrr!" roared the lion, and Mr. Smith
turned and fled. He wasn't very happy.
In fact, he was very unhappy.
And he was scared.

Mr. Smith thought he might have better luck on the other side of the river. He started to feel happier.

The hippopotamus just laughed.
Mr. Smith wasn't very happy. In fact, he
was very unhappy. And he was wet.

Mr. Smith decided to dry his clothes. But the monkey decided that she liked his clothes.

Mr. Smith wasn't very happy.
In fact, he was very unhappy. He had
no clothes. "At least she left my hat,"
he said. "I can wear that."

But the snake wouldn't let him.

But the elephant knew why. Then he grabbed Mr. Smith with his trunk…

and dumped him at the top of a tree. Mr. Smith wasn't very happy. In fact, he was very unhappy. He'd had enough. "I'm leaving," he said.

The animals waved good-bye as
Mr. Smith's ship sailed off.
They were very happy.
And so, at last, was Mr. Smith.